and PIMPLE POTION

ERIC
and the
PIMPLE POTION

BARBARA MITCHELHILL
Illustrated by Tony Ross

Andersen Press
LONDON

This edition published in Great Britain in 2019 by
Andersen Press Limited
20 Vauxhall Bridge Road
London SW1V 2SA
www.andersenpress.co.uk

First published in 1999 by Andersen Press Limited

2 4 6 8 10 9 7 5 3 1

British Library Cataloguing in Publication Data available.

ISBN 978 1 78344 827 2

Printed and bound in Great Britain
by Clays Limited, Elcograf S.p.A.

ONE

It was the worst day of Eric's life.

The suit Mum had ordered for him had arrived. It was unbelievable. Worse than any suit in the whole country. No – in the entire world!

It was bright blue satin with knickerbocker trousers. And he was supposed to wear it at Mum's wedding.

No way!

'But I want you to look special,' said Mum. 'Go on, duck. Try it on. Just to please me.'

He gave in – but first he closed the living-room curtains. Then he slipped into the satin suit.

'Oh, Eric!' said Mum, as tears filled her eyes. 'You look lovely!' And she hugged him

1

to her chest until he felt faint from lack of oxygen.

'I'm ever so excited,' Mum said, releasing him at last. 'The bridesmaids' dresses came this morning, too. Oh, the girls are going to look gorgeous!'

Eric's face turned white as paper. 'Bridesmaids?' he said. 'I didn't know there were going to be girls at the wedding.'

Mum ruffled his hair. 'I told you,' she said. 'I'm having Kylie and Jade Partridge.'

Eric's brain couldn't cope. His mum was marrying his teacher. That was enough for anybody. Now two of the worst girls in his class were going to the wedding. It was too much!

'They'll be coming later to try on their dresses,' said Mum. 'No sneaking off to your room, Eric. I want you to stay and be sociable.'

It was a nightmare! All afternoon the girls ran up and down the stairs, trying on horrible pink satin dresses. They pranced and twirled in front of mirrors. They giggled non-stop and made stupid remarks.

'Are you going to be a bridesmaid, Eric?'

'Will you have flowers in your hair?'

'And lipstick?'

Eric stayed sitting in a corner, hiding behind his comic. It was a bad day! He couldn't wait for it to end.

'Imagine The Bodge marrying your mum, Eric!'

'Will you call him "Daddy" or "Sir"?'

Eric said nothing. He was too depressed.

He was grateful to hear a loud rap at the front door. 'I'll get it!' he said, leaping up and escaping into the hall.

When he opened the door, a delivery man was standing on the step.

'Parcel for Braithwaite,' he said.

The package was from South America. Eric could tell by the stamps. Auntie Rose must have sent it. This was not good news. Somehow, her presents always got him into trouble.

But this time, he was in luck. The parcel was addressed to Mrs Christine Braithwaite. Eric breathed a sigh of relief

and put it on the telephone table. It was for Mum. She could look at it later.

It was then that he glanced up at the hall mirror and saw something on the tip of his nose. He leaned forward to get a better look. It was a small pink pimple. Could it be chickenpox?

Chickenpox would be good. Chickenpox would mean he'd miss the wedding. His heart jumped at the thought of it.

No blue satin suit!

No Partridge twins!

He could spend all day watching TV. Excellent!

He pressed his nose against the mirror and smiled.

TWO

'A parcel from Auntie Rose?' Mum said when everyone had gone. 'She must have sent me a present. Let's take a look.'

She tore off the brown paper and found a small, round pot and a letter which read:

Dear Christine,

I'll do my best to be home for your wedding but there have been terrible floods here and I had to stay for several days in a village above flood level. The family I stayed with gave me this little pot of cream. They say this potion has magical qualities — but then everyone here seems to believe in magic. Even that stone I sent Eric was supposed to be magic! Ha ha!

I was told that this is a fantastic skin cream and will make you very attractive to the opposite sex. So I thought it would be a nice present for your wedding. It might even make wrinkles disappear! You could try it. You never know!

Love and kisses to you and Eric (and Brian, of course!)

Hope to see you soon.

Rose x

Mum picked up the jar. 'Fancy!' she said, twisting the top and lifting it off.

Once the jar was opened, the smell of goats' droppings filled the room. To Eric, it was a familiar smell. Some time ago, Auntie Rose had sent Eric a magic jumper – the Striped Horror – and it had smelled just the same.

'Ugh!' said Mum wrinkling her nose. 'I can't put that on my face. Brian would hate it!'

Eric shrugged. 'It's not bad,' he said. 'He'll get used to it.'

'I don't think so,' said Mum, replacing the lid. 'Come on. Let's have tea. Brian's coming round later to talk about the wedding.'

Brian was known as The Bodge at school. He was not nearly as bad as everybody thought but, even so, Eric didn't want to stay in. There was always a chance he'd check Eric's homework.

'I promised to meet Wez,' he said. 'We've got a big match next week. We need loads of practice.'

Mum smiled. 'All right, duck. But don't be late back, will you?'

By the time Eric got to the rec, Wez was already running up and down, perfecting his dribbling.

'What's up, Ez?' said Wez as he aimed at an imaginary goal. 'You look about as cheerful as a squashed hedgehog.'

Eric sighed. 'Bad news,' he said. 'The suit arrived today and it's blue satin with knickerbockers!'

'That's real bad news,' said Wez, picking up the ball.

'And Mum's having bridesmaids.'

'Who?'

'The Partridge twins!'

'No!' said Wez, his eyes wide in disbelief. 'That's gruesome!'

Eric nodded gloomily.

'I've got to look after them at the reception,' he said, and struck the ground with the toe of his trainer. 'I tell you, Wez – I'm fed up. I've got to bunk off this wedding, somehow.'

Wez shook his head. 'I don't see how.'

Eric pointed to the pimple. 'Take a look at my face, will you? Can you see anything?'

Wez peered closely at Eric. 'A bit of dirt,' he said. 'Nothing unusual.'

'No! This!' said Eric, frantically tapping his nose. 'I thought it might be chickenpox. What do you think?'

'No, Ez. It's nothing like chickenpox. It's just an ordinary pimple. My brother's got 'em all over his face.'

But Eric shook his head and refused to believe it. He had a hunch that the pimple was going to be his salvation.

THREE

By the time Monday came, the pimple had grown. Eric examined it in the bathroom mirror and smiled. It looked like a pink mountain with a yellow peak. It was a beauty! Best of all, there were signs of three others on his chin. Just as he had thought, he had an infectious disease. It was only a matter of time before his mum noticed and sent for the doctor.

'Come on, Eric,' Mum called. 'I've got to be in town for nine o'clock. I'll give you a lift to school if you like.'

Eric clattered down the stairs and burst into the kitchen. 'I think I might be seriously ill,' he panted, pointing to the pimple.

Mum raised an eyebrow. 'Oh yes?' she said, and lifted his chin. 'Got any more like this?'

Eric peered down his shirt and looked carefully. No spots.

'Temperature?' she said, holding her hand to his forehead.

He tried thinking 'hot' – but it didn't work.

Mum shrugged her shoulders and reached for her coat. 'It's just your first day back after half term, duck. You'll be all right.'

'But it might be chickenpox!' he said in desperation.

Mum shook her head. 'No, Eric. Not chickenpox. You had that when you were three.'

Eric's stomach sank. His plan had failed dismally. How was he going to get out of the wedding now?

Wez sympathised as they went into school. 'You can think of something else,' he said. 'How about losing your memory . . . or running away to sea . . . or breaking your leg?'

But nothing appealed. Doom!

When Eric walked into the classroom that morning, a group of girls was huddled in the corner, giggling. The Partridge twins were in the middle and he knew they were up to something.

'He's here,' he heard Kylie whisper. Then the girls turned and looked over their shoulders.

'Not wearing the blue satin suit today?' Annie Barnstable called across to him. (She was the worst girl in the class. She was even worse than the Partridge twins.)

Eric ignored her but she didn't stop.

'We're all going to come to the Registry Office to see you. You'll look a real wimp.'

They burst out laughing and Eric turned purple. He wanted to shout something back but he didn't. The rest of the class was coming in through the door. He just hoped nobody else had heard what she had said.

No such luck. Brent Dwyer, the class bully, had ears like a bat.

'What's that about you and a blue satin suit?' he said as he passed Eric's desk. 'Are you in a panto, or what?' Then he gave him a punch on the shoulder and walked on, laughing.

Notes were passed round during maths and by break the whole class knew about the blue satin suit. It was a great joke to everybody – except Eric.

At breaktime, he and Wez went for a walk round the football pitch to get away from the giggles, but Brent Dwyer and his gang followed them.

'There goes Little Boy Blue!' Brent yelled after him.

'Get lost!' Eric called over his shoulder.

'Ooooooh!' said Annie Barnstable.

'Baby's got a real temper.'

'It's the ginger hair,' said Brent. 'And the pimples. Have you seen 'em on his chin? And he's got a massive one on the end of his nose.'

Eric had had enough. He spun round, crazy with rage, and lunged for Brent's legs. Brent was caught off-guard and he staggered back and fell with a thud onto the grass. Eric flung himself on top of him.

But not for long. Brent flipped Eric over on his back and caught him a bruiser on his left eye. The fight was in full swing and Annie Barnstable and the rest of the gang were whooping with delight.

'WHAT ON EARTH'S GOING ON?' The voice of The Bodge bellowed across the field as he stormed towards them. 'STOP THAT AT ONCE!' he yelled.

Eric's stomach tightened as he struggled free and wiped the blood from his nose. Now he was for it. The Bodge would tell Mum and she'd go crazy. Life couldn't get worse.

But it did – that afternoon during the art lesson.

FOUR

They had art every Monday afternoon.

'Today, I want you to paint a picture of a friend,' said The Bodge. 'Someone in your class. Put in plenty of detail – hair, eyes, clothes. Make it as interesting as you can.'

He smiled one of his 'new' smiles. (He never used to smile. Not until he went soppy over Eric's mum.)

'Don't make too much noise. I've got some marking to do,' he said. 'I'll look at your pictures at the end of the lesson.'

They got out the paints and easels and began. The Bodge watched out of the corner of his eye while he put red ticks and crosses on a pile of maths books.

There was only a faint murmur in the room and an occasional titter. Not enough to bother a teacher.

Eric did a brilliant picture of Wez with his fishing rod. And Wez did a fantastic one of Eric in his football gear. He even drew a football under his arm and a silver prize winner's cup in his hand.

'Great!' said Eric. 'Can I have it for my bedroom wall?'

'Course,' said Wez. 'If The Bodge lets us take 'em home.'

By then The Bodge had finished his marking and was putting the top on his pen. 'Time to pack away,' he said. 'Pin your paintings on the display boards and I'll come and look at them.'

It was at this point that the door burst open and the head teacher, Mrs Cracker (known as the Big Cheese), came in. 'Ah! Mr Hodgetts!' she said. 'I see you're having art.'

'Just finished,' he said. 'We've been doing portraits. Perhaps you'd like to have a look at our efforts, Mrs Cracker.'

She turned to the children and smiled. 'That would be nice.'

The drawing pins were out. The pictures were pinned on the wall. All thirty of them. Then Eric stared, wide-eyed. To his horror, more than half of them were of himself. Ginger hair . . . spotty face . . . a black eye . . . and a blue satin suit with knickerbocker trousers. He wanted to faint with shame.

'What's this?' the head teacher asked. 'Is it Dick Whittington?'

'It's Eric,' giggled Annie Barnstable. 'Wearing his outfit for the wedding.'

'We're going to be bridesmaids,' said the twins in unison.

Mrs Cracker coughed and looked at The Bodge. 'Hmm,' she said. 'Well, I'm sure you'll look very nice, dear. Very . . . er . . . unusual.' And she swept out of the room, quite forgetting to ask Mr Hodgetts whatever she had come to ask him in the first place.

When the bell went for home time, Eric rushed across the playground to get away from the other kids. He was through the gate in a flash. He didn't slow down until he was round the corner and halfway down Mill Street. Then he nipped into McNally's sweet shop to buy some chocolate. He needed something to cheer him up.

'If you don't mind me saying so, Eric,' said Mrs McNally as she took his money, 'you've got terrible spots.' She stared at his

chin and shook her head. 'It's your age, I
expect – but the chocolate will only make
'em worse, love. You'll soon be covered in
'em if you're not careful.' Then she smiled.
'Try an apple next time.'

Eric's shoulders slumped as he walked
towards the door. Filled with gloom, he tore
off the wrapping and bit into the chocolate.
So what if he did have the odd spot? That
was the least of his worries.

FIVE

Things were no better at home. When Mum saw his black eye, she went wild. 'Oh, Eric! You look terrible! How did that happen?'

Eric grunted something about crashing into a goalpost then quickly escaped upstairs to his bedroom.

At seven o'clock, The Bodge arrived. Mum hadn't been expecting him and she was washing her hair.

'Brian!' she said, wrapping a towel round her head. 'I thought it was your night for the photography club.' Eric was not pleased by this interruption. A film was starting on TV any minute.

'I think we should have a talk about Eric,' said The Bodge as he sat on the settee.

Eric shifted his gaze from the telly to The Bodge. Mum frowned, reached for the remote, and pressed the 'off' button. So much for the film!

The Bodge looked deadly serious. 'What's all this about a blue satin suit, Christine?' he said. 'The kids in my class are making Eric's life a misery. Isn't that right, Eric?'

Eric shuffled in his seat and shrugged.

'That fight with Brent Dwyer was about the suit, wasn't it?'

Eric said nothing and The Bodge turned back to Mum.

'You should see the paintings some of the kids did this afternoon. It's cruel, Christine. He shouldn't be made to wear something like that! It's ridiculous!'

Tears sprang up in Mum's eyes. 'It's a beautiful suit,' she said. 'He'll look gorgeous in it.'

She went upstairs and brought it down. 'See! It's lovely!'

The Bodge looked at the blue satin and the white frills and shook his head.

'He'll look silly, love,' he said. 'Can't you see? It's not right for a boy of his age.'

Mum pulled back her shoulders and stuck out her chin. Eric knew the signs. She was going to dig her heels in.

'I want him to wear it,' she said. 'It's my wedding – so there!'

The Bodge put an arm round Eric's shoulder.

'I was hoping Eric and I could wear the same kind of suit for the wedding,' he said.

'I think it's only right if he's going to be my Best Man.' Then he winked at Eric and said, 'Of course, I could always wear blue satin knickerbockers, I suppose.'

Mum's mouth started to twitch as she tried not to laugh. But she couldn't help it. She started giggling and that was that. She flung her arms round The Bodge and kissed him on the cheek. He had won. Eric was going to have a navy blue suit and blue shirt. Not exactly cool – but OK.

There was more good news that evening. They were all watching the film, eating choc ices out of the freezer, when the phone rang. Mum went to answer it and came back with a worried frown on her face.

'That was Allison Partridge – the twins' mum.'

'What's wrong?' asked The Bodge.

'It's her youngest, Ryan,' she said.

'In Miss Allan's class?'

'Yes. He's off school with chickenpox and now it looks as if Kylie's got it. Jade's sure to follow. Allison's decided to keep them both off school.'

Eric swallowed the last piece of choc ice. 'Does that mean they can't be bridesmaids?' he said.

'I'm afraid so,' said Mum.

Eric could hardly contain himself.

He was bursting with joy. He wanted to leap up. He wanted to fling his arms in the air and shout 'YES!' at the top of his voice. Instead he spread his hand across his mouth to hide his smile and turned back to watch the telly.

SIX

When Eric went up to bed that night and looked in the bathroom mirror, he didn't like what he saw: one black eye and – horror! – *five* pimples on his chin. The black eye would fade but the pimples might get even worse.

'A Best Man can't have spots,' he said to his reflection. 'I'd better do something about it.'

He opened the bathroom cabinet and looked at some of Mum's stuff.

There were only three things that might be any good. There was a bottle of moisturiser but he didn't think moisture would get rid of pimples.

There was a small packet marked 'Face Mask – for dry skin' – no good. (Eric had seen his mum with a face mask on. He didn't fancy being cast in concrete.)

The last thing was the pot of face cream from Auntie Rose. Eric took it down. He remembered Auntie Rose's letter. 'They say this potion has magical qualities . . .' she had written. 'It might even make wrinkles disappear.' In that case, thought Eric, getting rid of spots should be easy. He'd give it a try.

He took the pot to his bedroom. He changed into his pyjamas, got into bed and spread a thick layer of the cream on his face. Then he laid his head carefully on the pillow and closed his eyes. The smell of the potion was terrible but if it worked its magic, it would be worth the suffering.

*

In the morning when he woke up, not only had his pimples gone, but his black eye had disappeared, too! Only a vague smell of goats' droppings remained. Magic! Unfortunately, the potion had other effects . . . but Eric didn't find that out until later.

It was at school that Eric first noticed something odd about the way the girls were behaving. Instead of ignoring him or making rude remarks as usual, they were looking at him with big gooey eyes and smiling as he passed.

He became decidedly nervous. Even Wez noticed he wasn't his usual self.

'What's up, Ez?' he said.

'The girls,' said Eric. 'They're staring at me. Do I look weird or something?'

Wez checked Eric from head to foot and shook his head. 'You look a bit cleaner than usual. Apart from that, you look OK.'

Things didn't get better. Later, Eric found a note inside his desk with 'To Eric from Annie' written in pink felt tip. He felt sick. What was Annie Barnstable up to now? He didn't want to open it. But he couldn't stop himself.

Dear Eric...
I think u r really cool.
Meet me behind the bike shed
after dinner.
Will you be my boyfriend?
I love you,

Annie

XXXXXXXXXXXXXXXXXXXX
XXXXXXXXXXXXXXXXXXXX
XXXXXXXXXXXXXXXXXXXX

Annie Barnstable? No! This was a joke, right? His face flushed crimson. He frowned and screwed up the note. He stared across the class, only to see Annie staring back with a moonstruck expression. She was smiling and wiggling her fingers in a silly kind of wave. Eric turned away at once. It couldn't be true! The WORST GIRL ON EARTH was crazy about him!

SEVEN

After a long discussion with Wez, Eric decided he'd have to hide out during the lunchbreak. Whatever Annie Barnstable was up to, he had to avoid her. In the end, he decided he would go to the boiler room. It was dark and very dirty. No girl would want to follow him there. It was perfect.

The boiler room was interesting in a weird kind of way – pipes and clocks and wheels. Eric enjoyed looking at them and finding out where they went. Unfortunately, by the time the bell went for afternoon lessons, he was filthy.

As he hurried towards class, someone shouted, 'Eric Braithwaite! What have you been up to?' It was the Big Cheese. 'You look as if you've been down a coalmine!

Go and wash at once. As for your jumper –
it's ruined!'

Eric gave a watery smile and said, 'Yes,
Miss,' and hurried past with his head
down. Even Mrs Cracker's anger was worth
it. He had escaped A.B. That was all that
mattered.

Throughout that afternoon, Annie
gazed across the classroom with sad,
droopy eyes. She even sent him notes but
he tore them up and dropped them on the
floor. He had to be tough. He'd ignore
her completely and think about the school
football match. Today's was a big one –
North Street School against Kirstall Road.
He had to be on top form. He had to be
FOCUSED.

*

After school, Eric got changed into his
football kit.

'How many goals will you score today,
Ez?' shouted one of the team.

'Dunno,' said Eric modestly. 'Three or four maybe.'

The North Street team cheered, 'You're the best, Ez!' As they ran out onto the pitch, Eric noticed something odd.

Most of the girls from his class were standing on the sidelines. What was going on? They never came to matches. Most of them hated football. He felt a strange uneasy prickle at the back of his neck. Then he heard . . .

'Give us an E . . . Give us an R . . . Give us an I . . . Give us a C . . . What have we got? ERIC!' The girls jumped in the air, waving and cheering, as if he were some kind of superhero.

Even the Kirstall Road team thought it was a laugh.

'Got a fan club, have you, Ez?'

'Did you pay 'em to come?'

But once the game began, things got worse. The girls cheered and screamed every time Eric got near the ball. It was so embarrassing that Eric couldn't concentrate. His passes were pathetic and he missed several easy shots at goal. In the end, they lost the match. Kirstall Road 7, North Street 0. No wonder!

The home team were not pleased with him.

'Forgotten how to play football, Eric?' one of them said as they stormed off the pitch.

'Stop messing about with the girls,' said another. 'You've gone soft!'

Only Wez would speak to him, after that.

'I wouldn't mind having fans,' he said, as they walked home.

'Well, I don't want 'em!' said Eric. 'Why can't they ignore me like usual?'

Wez shook his head. He had no idea.

'They're driving me crazy! I try not to think about it but I even imagine they're following me.'

Wez glanced over his shoulder.

'You're not imagining it, Ez. They *are* following you.'

Eric spun round. He was right! Annie Barnstable and four other girls were twenty metres or so behind.

Then Wez began to shake with laughter. 'You know, Ez,' he said, 'they must think you're dead attractive. Like one of the film stars. The girls can't leave you alone.'

'That's stupid! Why should they suddenly fancy me? I don't understand . . .'

He stopped mid-sentence as he remembered Auntie Rose's letter. *They say this potion has magical qualities . . . It will make you very attractive to the opposite sex.* Eric groaned. He should have guessed. Everything Auntie Rose sent caused trouble. The pot of cream was no exception.

Slowly, he explained everything to Wez. 'So now what do we do?' he said. 'I don't want all this girl rubbish. We've got to STOP it.'

Wez was silent while he thought. 'I've read a bit about magic and stuff,' he said at last. 'What you do is bathe in running water in moonlight.'

'You mean have a bath?'

'No. You've got to have a river or something . . . It can't be tap water.'

'Why?'

'Dunno. You've got to take all your

clothes off and wash the magic off. That's the rules.'

Eric looked back. The girls were still following and getting closer.

'Right then. I can't think of anything else to do, so I'll give it a try. Let's hope it works.'

With that, they arranged to meet near the brook behind Denver Street.

'At midnight,' said Eric. 'And don't be late.'

EIGHT

Eric's problem was staying awake. He put several apples and a couple of books in his bed to stop himself getting too comfortable. And just in case he dropped off, he tied a piece of string from his big toe to the chest of drawers. He had seen that in a cartoon on the telly.

When his watch showed quarter to twelve, he untied the string, slipped out of bed and crept downstairs. Then he left by the back door and headed for Denver Street. A full moon! Excellent! He reached the brook and stood waiting, hoping Wez wouldn't be late.

He arrived five minutes after Eric. He was wearing wellies and carrying a yellow plastic bucket.

'What have you brought that for?' Eric hissed.

Wez smiled mysteriously. 'Think about it, Ez,' he said. 'The brook's only a few centimetres deep. You're supposed to bathe in it – not paddle.'

'So?'

'So I'll fill the bucket from the brook and pour the water over your head. That should do it! Brilliant, eh?'

The night was cold and Eric wanted to get Wez's plan over with as soon as possible.

'Are you sure I've got to be naked?' he asked as he pulled off his sweater.

'Sure,' said Wez. 'It won't work if you're not.'

Grumbling under his breath, Eric dropped all his clothes on the bank. He stood there shivering, his arms wrapped round his chest, his skin luminous and silver in the moonlight.

'IT'S FREEZING!'

'Sssh!' said Wez. 'You'll wake the neighbours.'

Eric grimaced and waded reluctantly into the brook. Wez followed behind, dipping his bucket in the water.

Unluckily for Eric, the water in the brook was not crystal clear. So the bucket also contained mud, frogspawn and slimy green weed.

'Bend down a bit,' said Wez cheerfully, 'and I'll pour.'

And Eric – who was now too cold to speak – did as he was told. As he crouched there, Wez lifted the bucket over Eric's head and let the murky water cascade over him.

'That should do it,' said Wez and Eric raised himself like a weed-covered spectre out of the water.

It was then that the beam of a torch flashed across the brook. The boys turned and peered into the gloom. Someone was on the bank.

Wez had water in his eyes and couldn't see who it was. But Eric could see well enough. It was the last person on earth he wanted to see. It was Annie Barnstable!

'It's you, isn't it, Eric?' she called out in a soppy voice. 'I saw you from my bedroom

window. You came to see me after all! I knew you liked me really.'

Eric clung to Wez and hid behind him, trying to make himself invisible.

Suddenly, the torchlight landed on his bare flesh and Annie Barnstable let out a scream. There were a few seconds of silence that seemed to stretch into hours . . . and then they heard her burst into gales of laughter.

'Look at you!' she bawled. 'No clothes on and covered in slime. What do you think you're doing, Eric Braithwaite? I can't wait to tell everybody tomorrow. Maybe I should go and get my phone and take a picture.'

Before she had a chance to move, the boys leaped for the bank. Eric grabbed his clothes and shot up Denver Street like a wild thing. Luckily, there was no one about. Even in Corporation Street, the only thing he saw was next door's cat on the prowl.

Once he was back in his room, he flung himself onto his bed and lay there panting and dripping in weeds and water. It was all too much. Why was life so difficult? He wrapped the duvet round him and closed his eyes. Then, as he drifted off to sleep, nightmares filled his head of what might happen next day at school.

NINE

As Eric walked through the school gates the next morning, he saw a group of kids gathered round Brent Dwyer. One of them was Annie Barnstable. When he was level with them, she spotted him and they all turned.

'Hiya, Eric,' she sneered. 'Learned to play football yet, wimp?'

Eric was taken aback. Was this Annie Barnstable, who had sent him love notes?

'You're useless,' she said. 'Get real, Eric. Stop acting like a drip.'

Did she say 'drip'? Was she going to say something about last night in the brook? Or seeing him naked?

But no. Annie Barnstable just stuck out

her tongue at Eric and carried on talking to
Brent Dwyer.

'She's back to normal!' said Eric. 'What
happened?'

'The moonlight and the water worked. That's what happened,' said Wez, feeling smug. 'She doesn't even remember last night. You see – those books were right. The power of reading, Ez!'

Eric grinned. He couldn't believe his luck. 'Yeah! It worked all right. Now I can forget about girls and you can help me with my speech.'

'What speech?'

'My speech at the wedding. The Best Man always gives a speech. Got any ideas, Wez?'

'No,' said Wez. 'But there is one thing I've noticed . . . '

'What?'

'You've got that pimple on the end of your nose again. If you want, I can get you some of my brother's spot cream.'

Eric shook his head. 'Thanks . . . but no thanks. What's one pimple in my difficult life, Wez? Safer to leave it alone.'

Much safer.

ERIC
and the
STRIPED HORROR

BARBARA MITCHELHILL
Illustrated by Tony Ross

Eric is more sporty than brainy, but a big test is
looming. Then his auntie sends him a very strange
present: an ugly, stinky, stripy jumper with magical
powers. It can turn the wearer into a genius.
Will it work on him?

978 1 78344 796 1

ERIC
and the
WISHING STONE

BARBARA MITCHELHILL
Illustrated by Tony Ross

Eric is just no good at tests and schoolwork.
His mum isn't happy and decides he needs
extra lessons with his grumpy teacher Mr
Hodgetts, much to Eric's horror. So when a
mysterious magic stone
arrives, Eric hopes it
can grant his biggest
wish of all . . .

978 1 78344 797 8